Mama's
Little Bears

by Nancy Tafuri

SCHOLASTIC PRESS • NEW YORK

One spring day,
Little Bears were fishing
with their Mama.

Little Bears
fished and fished . . .

until . . .

off they ran!

What's over there?

What's under here?

What's in there?

What's down here?

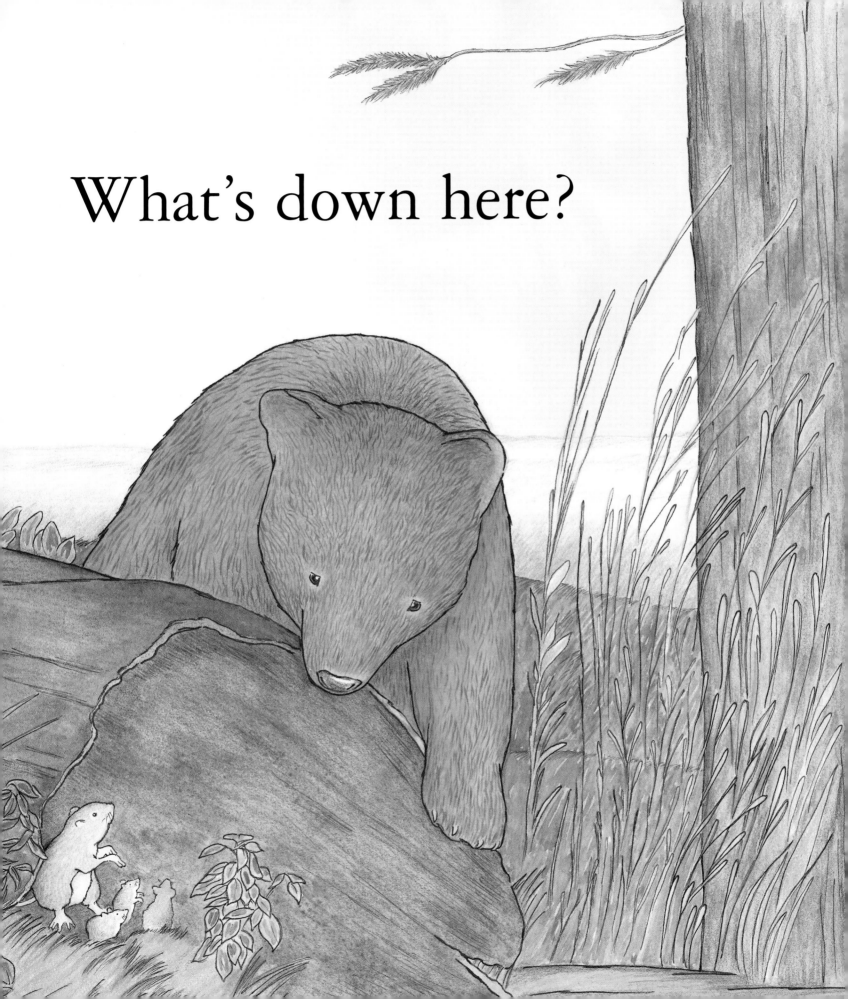

What's up there?

Little Bears
scurried

up,
up,
up.

Little Bears hurried

down, down, down.

MAMA!

And there she was!

Little Bears hugged
their Mama so tight . . .

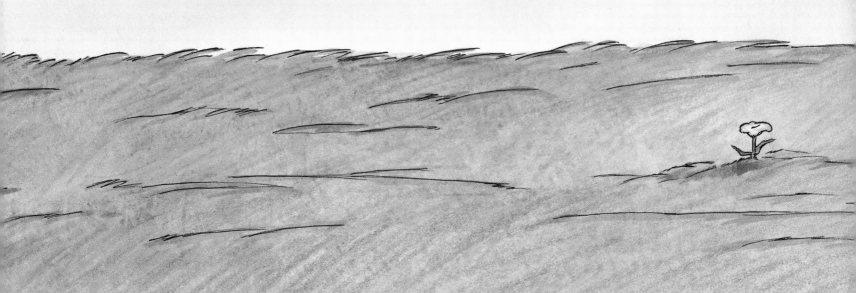

and Mama Bear hugged
them right back!

LIBRARY OF CONGRESS CATALOGING-IN-PUBLICATION DATA
Tafuri, Nancy.
Mama's Little Bears / by Nancy Tafuri.— 1st ed.   p. cm.
Summary: The Little Bears explore their forest home but never stray too far from their Mama.
ISBN 0-439-27311-0   [1.Bears–Fiction. 2. Mother and child–Fiction.] I. Title.
PZ7.T117 Mam 2002   [E]--dc21   2001020935

10 9 8 7 6 5 4 3 2 1   02 03 04 05 06
Printed in Singapore   46   First edition, April 2002

Nancy Tafuri's art was rendered in watercolor paint and pastels. The text type was set in 54-point Garamond Three.
The display type was set in Goudy Handtooled. Book design by Nancy Tafuri and David Saylor

For Cristina